THIS **SWEET PICKLES**® **BOOK BELONGS TO**

_____

In the world of *Sweet Pickles,* each animal gets into a pickle because of an all too human personality trait.

This book is about Vain Vulture who thinks he is better than anyone else.

Books in the Sweet Pickles Series:

Library of Congress Cataloging in Publication Data

Hefter, Richard.
    Kiss me, I'm vulture.

    (Sweet Pickles series)
    SUMMARY: Vulture is so wrapped up in himself
that his friends decide to teach him a lesson.
    [1. Vultures—Fiction] I. Title. II. Series.
PZ7.H3587Ki   [E]   78-16268
ISBN 0-03-042071-7

Sweet Pickles is the registered trademark of
Perle/Reinach/Hefter.

Printed in the United States of America

Weekly Reader Books' Edition

Weekly Reader Books presents

KISS ME, I'M
VULTURE

Written and illustrated by
Richard Hefter
Edited by Ruth Lerner Perle

Holt, Rinehart and Winston · New York

Vulture was admiring himself in the mirror when
he overheard Lion talking to Walrus.

"Oh, dear," sighed Walrus. "We really have something
to worry about!"

"Don't be silly," smiled Lion. "It's easy.
All we have to do is find someone to lead the
Harvest Parade."

"Oh, my," moaned Walrus. "Why did we ever let ourselves get talked into organizing the parade? Suppose something goes wrong? Suppose it rains? What if nobody shows up to watch? Suppose it gets cold? And, worst of all, what if we can't find anybody to lead the parade?"

"Stop that worrying right now," sighed Lion.
"Everything will work out just fine. Everyone
is looking forward to the parade. All we need
to do now is find someone to stand out in front of
the parade in the costume and lead us down Main Street."

Vulture rushed over to them.
"I couldn't help overhearing your little problem,
friends," said Vulture. "Maybe I can help you find
just the right one to lead your parade."

"That's all right, Vulture," smiled Lion. "I don't think
we need any help."

"On the contrary," screeched Vulture, "help
is just what you need. You are obviously
having trouble making up your minds."

Vulture threw his arm around Walrus. "First," he said, "you need to find someone who is really impressive and handsome."

"Oh?" said Walrus.

"Yes!" cried Vulture. "Someone tall and strong and gorgeous."

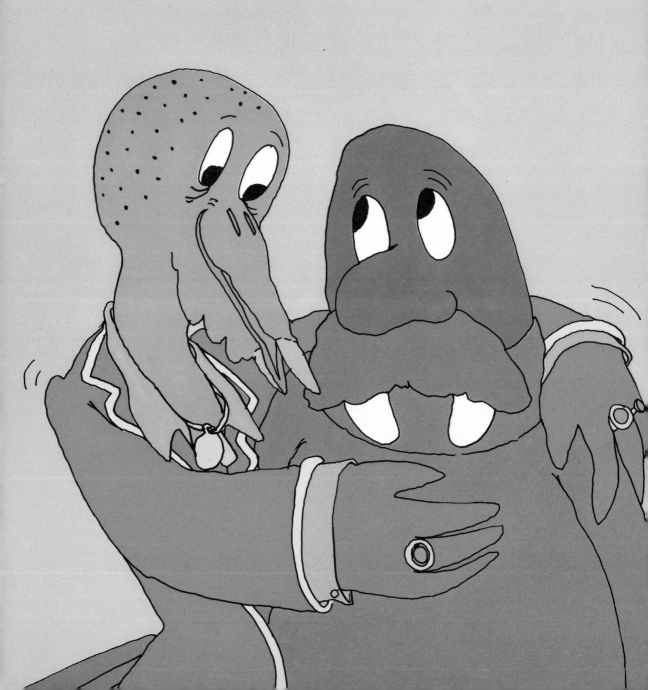

Vulture stood on his tippy toes and preened himself.
"You need a perfect specimen, a natural leader."
"But, Vulture," cried Lion. "It's just a parade."

Vulture jumped up and down in front of Lion.
"Just a parade!" he yelled. "Just a parade indeed!
That's the trouble around here. Nobody knows about
making an impression. You guys are all so ordinary.
What you need is someone *extra*ordinary."

Vulture looked into his mirror.
"Someone strong! Someone handsome! A shining example
to everyone. That's what you need to be the LEADER
of the parade."
"But Vulture," moaned Walrus, "where are we ever
going to find someone like that?"

"I know!" exclaimed Lion. "Camel is tall. Let's ask her to be the leader."

Vulture stretched himself up onto the tips of his toes.
Then he pulled his neck straight and made himself
as tall as he could.
"There!" he squawked. "See what I mean?
I mean TALL!"
"Gee," moaned Walrus, as he looked up at Vulture.
"Nobody in the whole town is THAT tall."

"How about handsome, then?" sighed Lion. "Maybe we could find someone handsome."

"Perfect," cooed Vulture. "Just perfect. You couldn't have picked a better quality. It's so important for you to find someone really handsome to lead the parade."

Vulture took out his mirror and began to admire himself. "And when it comes to handsome, you KNOW that there is no one around handsomer than......"

"Iguana!" shouted Lion. "With that long bumpy tail and her lovely green color, she's really handsome."

"NO, NO, NO!" screeched Vulture. "Iguana's all right—but I mean really HANDSOME!"

Vulture held himself straight, puffed out his chest and smiled his most dazzling Vulture smile. "See what I mean!" he shouted.

"Oh, dear," groaned Walrus, "nobody in town is THAT handsome. What are we going to do?"

"Hippo is impressive," smiled Lion. "And Elephant is strong."

"Not as impressive as this!" shouted Vulture.
"And not as strong as THIS!" Then he grabbed
Lion and lifted him off the ground.
"How about *this* for strong!"
"You put me down right now!" yelled Lion.

Vulture put Lion down.
"I know," cried Walrus, "let's ask Rabbit to lead
the parade. He dresses very well and always
looks so neat."

"NO! NO! NO!" screamed Vulture. "You can't be serious. You call that well dressed? All Rabbit ever wears is a plain blue suit and a red tie. What you need is someone with STYLE and CLASS!"

Vulture pulled off his red jacket.
"Look at that jacket!" he screeched. "Look at the
green lining. Look at the yellow piping! That's style.
That is class. Why, there is no one in this
whole town with a sense of clothing as good as this.
NO ONE AROUND HERE DRESSES AS
BEAUTIFULLY AS I DO!"

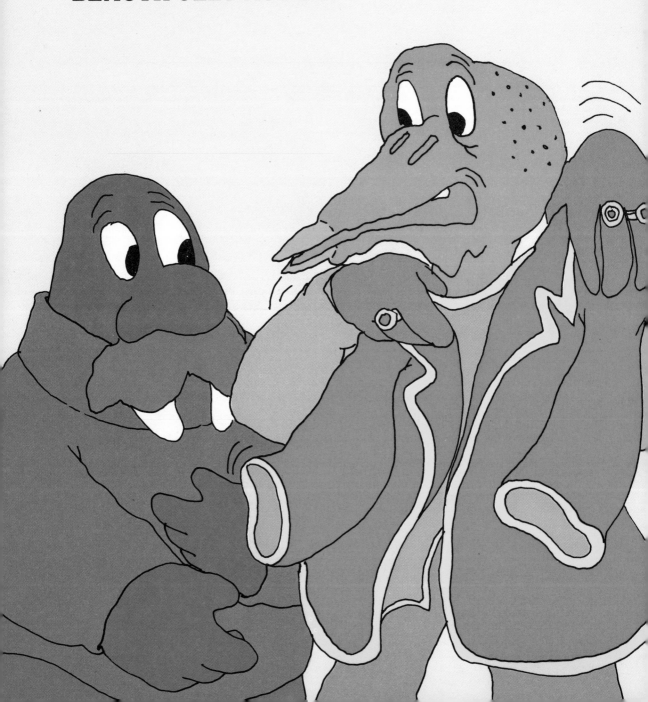

Vulture jumped up and down.
"NO ONE IN THIS WHOLE TOWN
IS AS HANDSOME AS I AM!" he shouted.
"AND NO ONE IS TALLER OR
STRONGER OR MORE IMPRESSIVE OR MORE
GORGEOUS! OOH, I COULD JUST KISS ME!"

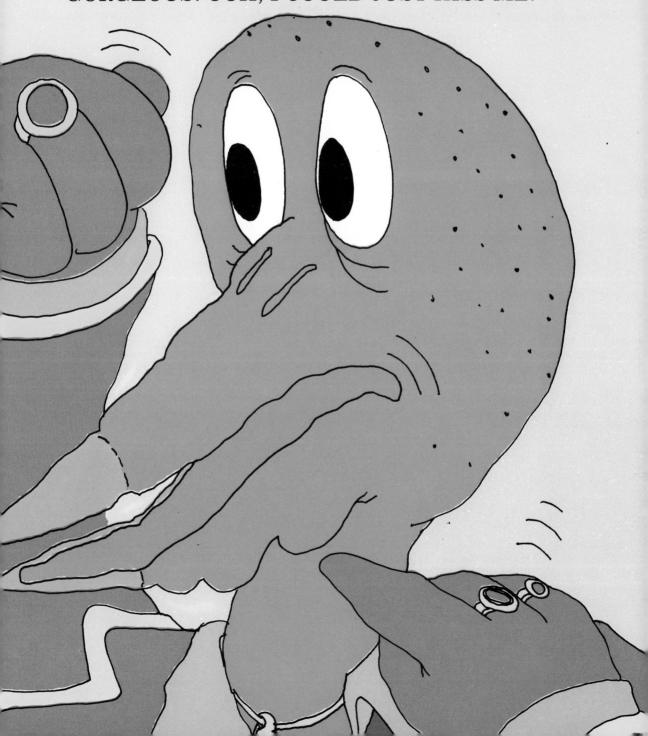

Vulture looked straight at Lion and Walrus.
He began to shout again.
"I AM THE GREATEST AND THE MOST
BEAUTIFUL AND THE MOST WONDERFUL
ONE IN THIS OR ANY OTHER TOWN AND
THERE IS NO ONE ELSE YOU CAN POSSIBLY
CHOOSE TO LEAD THE BIG PARADE!"
Vulture sat down.

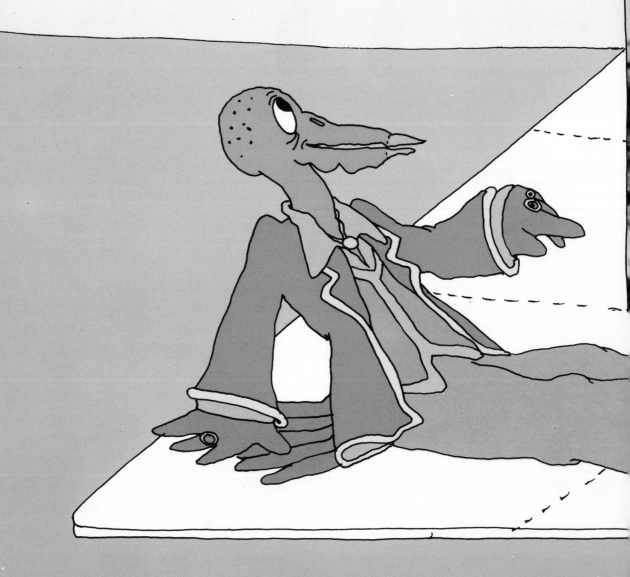

"Oh, dear," groaned Walrus. "If you feel that way about it, I guess it will be all right to let you lead the parade."

"Are you sure you want to?" asked Lion.
"You will have to wear the leader's costume, you know."

"Is there any doubt left in your mind?" cackled Vulture. "Show me my leader's costume and I'll show you how the most beautiful creature in town leads a parade!"

Lion and Walrus rushed off to get Vulture's parade costume.

All along Main Street, folks started to gather for the big parade.

Elephant brought her trumpet. Rabbit had his drum.
Goose and Moose and Yak were carrying a big banner.
Turtle brought her flute.
Everyone was all dressed up. Everyone was
clean and shiny. Even Nightingale looked her best.

"We're all ready to march!" cried Rabbit.
"Unfurl the banners! Strike up the band!
Let's get going."
"Wait, wait," puffed Walrus as he came running up.
"Wait for the leader...he's coming now!"
"*Boom, Booom, Boom!*" Rabbit banged his drum.
"TARARARAH," Elephant played her trumpet.

Yak and Moose and Goose spread out their banner.
It said: THE GREAT ANNUAL
SWEET PICKLES HARVEST PARADE.

"What a wonderful idea for a parade!" exclaimed
Quail. "But where is the leader?"

"Look!" cried Lion. "Here he comes now!"

Vulture came waddling around the corner.
He was wearing his costume.
He was dressed as a giant tomato.
He was completely hidden inside the giant tomato.
There was nothing showing but his beak and his feet.
"HOORAY!" shouted everyone.
The parade started.

"How did I ever get myself into this?"
grumbled Vulture from inside the tomato.
"How could this happen to me?"
"You are just a natural leader I guess," smiled Lion.

"You're right!" exclaimed Vulture from inside the tomato. "And I'm the handsomest, tallest, strongest, most impressive, best dressed tomato you'll ever see!"

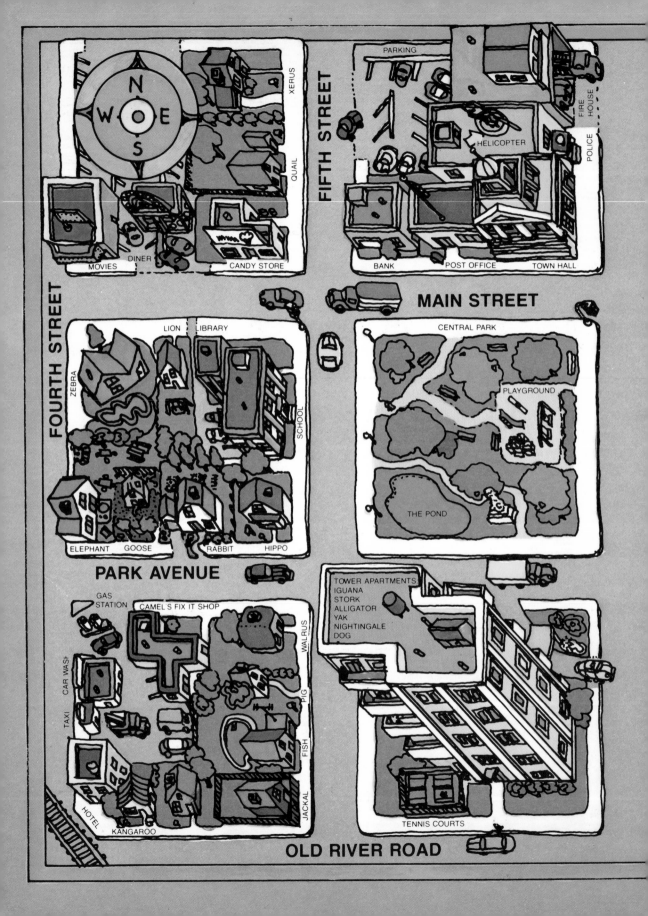